Introduction

From 2017 the syllabus for the AMusTCL has some significant changes from the previous version. For full and up-to-date details of the current syllabus you should refer to Trinity's website, www.trinitycollege.com/music, but the following summary may help:

Section A – Written Skills is unchanged from the previous syllabus.

Section B – Prescribed Works contains questions on five set works, matching the periods included in Section A. For each set work candidates may either write a single essay or answer a series of questions requiring shorter answers.

Section C is no longer included.

From 2017 candidates must answer a total of five questions, including at least one question from Section A and at least one question from Section B.

This study guide concentrates exclusively on Section A. For advice and guidance on Section B you may download free of charge the material published on Trinity College London's website. This has been updated to accommodate the new syllabus.

Anyone who wishes may enter AMusTCL: there are no formal prerequisites. However, in order to succeed you need to begin your preparation having a thorough grounding in academic music such as is required for admission to a university or conservatoire. This will mean that you know and can write chord progressions in all major and minor keys, making idiomatic use of chords derived from triads and sevenths, chromatic chords such as the major triad and seventh on the supertonic, Neapolitan and augmented sixths and diminished sevenths. You also should have a good grounding in musical history and analysis. There is more specific guidance about this in the various sections which follow and in the material published on the website.

With what has just been described as your starting point you should find that, with the further guidance of a qualified teacher, the materials in this book and on the website provide the necessary support to help ensure your success in the exam. Working from this Study Guide and the material on the website is not a substitute for study that is guided by a teacher; rather, it is a tool for use with a teacher.
In order to pass the AMusTCL diploma you need to be at the standard expected of undergraduate students as they complete their first year of study: basic professional competence on which to build towards graduation a couple of years later. Put another way, if you still struggle to recognise the key in which a piece of music is written or to say where a modulation has occurred, if you cannot readily say what qualities make a piece typical of the time when it was written, or if it takes you more than a minute to write a simple cadence with an approach chord correctly, then you still have some preparatory study to complete before you are ready to begin to work for AMusTCL.

We wish you well in your preparation and look forward to seeing your work in due course.

AMusTCL

Section A – Written Musical Skills

Questions will require candidates to write melody, harmony or counterpoint according to the stylistic conventions of various historical periods or to orchestrate according to such conventions. Four periods have been identified and for each there will be at least one question.

Candidates should note that in some cases the musical extracts used in questions may begin and end in different keys. Unless stated otherwise in the descriptions below, the material given may include one complete part or a selection of phrases from two or more parts. The intention will be to lead candidates towards producing work that is musical. The amount that may be left for candidates to complete in its entirety at the end of a question will depend on the style of the music in a particular question.

The periods and types of question are as follows:

Period 1 – Baroque (before c.1760): Lutheran Chorale

The chorale, typically but not exclusively composed by J S Bach, will **not** be in triple time and will consist of four phrases, in a diatonic major or minor key.

> The first phrase is given fully harmonised as by the composer.
>
> The second and third phrases are given melody only: candidates are asked to write idiomatic parts for alto, tenor and bass, using short score.
>
> The final phrase is blank: candidates are asked to write all four parts, maintaining the style as modelled in the first phrase and ending in the tonic key.

Period 2 – Classical (c.1760-1810): Orchestration

A short passage from a work written in this period will be set. Candidates are asked to orchestrate selected parts of the passage for specified instrumental groups including full orchestra. The instruments specified will be restricted to those used by composers active during the period.

Period 3 – Early Romantic (c.1810-1860): Pianoforte

Part or all of a work for solo pianoforte will be given, starting as originally written. The opening will be given in full. Thereafter there will be an indication of how the music might proceed. The candidate is asked to continue the piece at their discretion in the same style, working towards a final cadence.

Period 4 – Twentieth Century: Popular Song *and/or* Melodic Composition

Popular Song: Part or all of a song for voice and piano in popular style will be set. The passage might not be the start of the song (e.g. it could be the refrain) and some of the music will be given in full as in the original. Elsewhere, to indicate how the music should continue, one part in its entirety or phrases from both voice and piano parts may be provided. Candidates should complete the music in the appropriate idiom using the chord indications provided, including the final cadence and its approach in full.

Melodic Composition: A fragment of melody, taken from a non-diatonic twentieth century work will be set. Candidates should continue this to create a coherent and complete short piece of music for a solo single-line instrument of 24-30 bars. To answer this question successfully candidates will need to use some other system than tonal harmony as the basis of their work.

For requirements and support for Section B and for full guidance on the AMusTCL diploma please visit www.trinitycollege.com/music

Period 1: Baroque

In order to write well in the style of a Lutheran chorale you need these pre-requisites:

- a thorough knowledge of tonal harmony, including secondary sevenths, diminished sevenths, all forms of decoration and the usual chromatic chords
- awareness of the conventions of chorale singing as it was done in the performance of cantatas and settings of the passion during the late 17th and early 18th centuries
- a thorough grasp of the conventions of chorale harmonisation, particularly as exemplified in the work of JS Bach.

The best way to learn the second and third of these pre-requisites is from taking part in performances of cantatas and settings of the Passion composed in the later years of the baroque period. If this is not possible, then you should study scores of some of these works along with recordings made by people who try to render the music authentically. Resources for this are readily available throughout the world and may be easily located via the internet. All serious students of music should be gradually building a library of written and recorded material to which they can refer whenever necessary.

Harmonising a Lutheran Chorale

The chorale melodies of the Lutheran (Protestant) Church come from a variety of sources and the harmonisation of these was a major preoccupation of J S Bach. Luther, like Bach, composed many of the tunes and adapted medieval hymns and folksongs and it was from this vast collection of four-part harmonised hymn tunes that much of the harmonic practice of Western music during the years c.1600–1900 was built. In the chorales, tonal organisation, chord selection, progression and spacing can be studied in miniature and then applied to large-scale tonal structures; as such, the chorales can be regarded as a starting point for the study of tonal harmony.

To prepare for this question with confidence candidates should be fluent in the use of diatonic harmony including the use of the dominant and diminished seventh chords and should be able to modulate to closely-related keys: they should also be skilful in the use of passing notes and suspensions, and in spacing parts for voices. Chromatic chords such as Neapolitan and augmented sixths are not common in chorale harmonisation but the use of both the secondary dominant and occasional chromatic alteration of the subdominant are encountered. Equipped with these skills the candidate should have no difficulty in tackling the chorale harmonisation question.

An example of the kind of question that will be set is given, followed by a version of the same chorale harmonised by J S Bach. Phrases from three other harmonisations of the same chorale, two by Bach and one attributed to J Crüger, will then be used to illustrate various aspects of chorale harmonisation and its characteristics. Finally, Bach's most ambitious setting of the chorale, from the *St Matthew Passion*, will be given in full.

Question: Continuing in the given style, add parts for alto, tenor and bass to the given melody and add a final phrase in four parts, concluding in the tonic key.

Example 1

J S Bach

Baroque: Lutheran Chorale

Example 2 — J S Bach Herzliebster Jesu (Riemenschneidner no. 78)

Firstly, let us consider the Bach harmonisation from a tonal point of view:

- The tonic key, B minor, is well defined in bars 1-3 with mostly a reiteration of tonic and dominant chords leading to an imperfect cadence.

- Bars 3-6 prepare for the modulation to D major (the relative major) which is finalised in bar 6, using the pivot chord which is IV7b in B minor and II7b in D major followed by a straightforward perfect cadence in the new key.

- Bars 7-9 touch on the subdominant of D major, G major and its relative, E minor, before cadencing on the dominant of B minor resolving into the final phrase in the home key.

Bach's chord selection reveals the use of a diminished seventh (**a**) and a judicious mix of root position and first inversion chords. Second inversion chords, of which there are none in this example, should be used sparingly and mainly as $^6_4$ $^5_3$ cadential formulae.[1] The final chord in this example illustrates the use of tierce de Picardie, raising the minor third of the tonic chord by a chromatic semitone to end with a major and not a minor chord.[2]

Much use is made of passing notes, the accented passing notes providing a certain astringency (**e**), and the unaccented passing notes contributing to the flowing vocal lines, particularly in the bass part.

The use of chords of the seventh, prepared concordantly, and the seventh itself, resolved downwards in the tenor parts (**b**), add richness to the part-writing, as does the suspension in the alto part (**c**), in this case made more effective by its ornamental resolution. Dominant sevenths, which do not need concordant preparation, resolve downwards by step and leading notes rise to their tonics except where, as in bars 10-11, the leading note moves onto the fifth of the following chord to add richness to the final statement.[3]

The tessitura of the tenor line is generally held above the stave; this leads to a balanced vocal sound. The overlapping of the tenor and bass parts (**d**) is generally not recommended unless, as here, the 'line' of the tenor part takes precedence.

---

1. One of the most common errors candidates make is to use second inversion chords in places where the great chorale harmonisers never used them.
2. It was extremely unusual for a minor key chorale to end on a minor chord; you should use a tierce de Picardie as a matter of course if your chorale is in a minor key.
3. The final chord of a cadence is almost always complete and this is often achieved by moving the leading note down a third to the dominant in either the alto or the tenor – but never in the soprano.

Example 3 — *attrib.* J Crüger

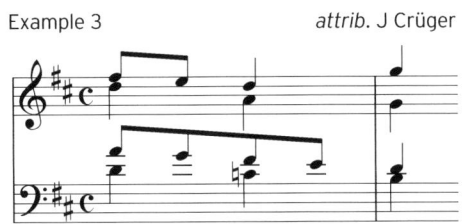

Example 4 — *attrib.* J Crüger

If we now compare two phrases from the Crüger harmonisation with the previous example, we note in bar 4 a passing modulation to G major adding a small chromatic embellishment (Example 3). In bar 8 the characteristic baroque pattern of progression from root to first inversion (and vice-versa) is evident with passing and chord notes (Example 4).

Example 5 — J S Bach

Example 6 — J S Bach

In another setting of this chorale by J S Bach (no. 59 in the Riemenschneider collection) bars 5–6 are treated more chromatically with the use of the subdominant with a flattened third on beat 2 and with the diminished seventh on the fourth beat (Example 5). The final phrase is similarly chromatic in its use of the diminished seventh (**a** in Example 6) and the secondary dominant on beat 3. It is also worth noting Bach's use of the passing six-four chord (**a** in Example 5) with the bass moving by step.

Bach's setting of this chorale in the *St Matthew Passion* is his richest in vocal texture and is quoted in full. The chromatic bass line in the first phrase and his use of passing notes and harmony notes together with the suspension in the penultimate bar contribute to the expressive nature of this setting.

Example 7 — J S Bach *St Matthew Passion*, Herzliebster Jesu

Baroque: Lutheran Chorale

Example 8

Example 9

Thus in these examples of harmonisation of the same chorale we encounter the whole vocabulary of chorale harmonisation and part-writing. A useful exercise would be to transpose the cadences, particularly those employing the II7b–V–I progression and its chromatic substitute, the secondary dominant, into a variety of keys.[4]

In passing, we should note as a general rule that augmented intervals resolve outwards and diminished intervals inwards (see Examples 8 and 9). Parallel fifths and octaves are sometimes avoided by the omission of the fifth of the chord, but largely by using contrary movement between the outside parts or by moving in parallel thirds and sixths.

The following openings, of the kind to be encountered in the exam, are taken from Riemenschneider's collection of 371 chorale harmonisations and the numbers refer to this collection.[5] When you have worked these examples through, compare them with those of Bach: there is no better teacher.[6]

N.B. Some of the examples are longer than will be used in exam papers, but they give useful practice material in the style.

Example 10
J S Bach Christus, der ist mein Leben (Riemenschneider no. 6)

---

4 Usually this chromatic chord includes a seventh.
5 *Alfred Riemenschneider, 371 Harmonised Chorales and 69 Chorale Melodies with Figured Bass by J S Bach* (Schirmer)
6 By way of reassurance, you should not forget that Bach was always setting particular words when he wrote his chorale harmonies (though often we no longer know what these words were) and the particular effects he used were chosen to give extra meaning to these words.

Baroque: Lutheran Chorale

Period 2: Classical

Roughly speaking, the Classical period in the history of Western music extends from 1770 to 1810.[1] It encompasses the mature works of Haydn (1732-1809) and Gluck (1714-1787), Mozart's entire output (1756-1791), the early works of Beethoven (1770-1827) and also the works of their contemporaries. Vienna was the centre for this style, though in all the major European capitals there were musicians who made strenuous efforts to match the elegance, grace and universality that are the hallmarks of classical aesthetics.

If you offer this period for the AMusTCL you will have to work an exercise in orchestration, based on a few bars drawn from original material from the period. In order to succeed in this you must be thoroughly conversant with elementary harmony, secondary sevenths, the higher dominant discords and the more usual chromatic chords. Although you will not be asked to harmonise anything in this section of the exam, you will be unable to write idiomatic parts for the instruments specified in the question if you cannot deal quickly and confidently with the conventions of harmonic movement.

---

1   You will note that an exercise later in this section comes from a work written by Schubert in 1813; this shows the flexibility of these dates.

Orchestration

The Classical Orchestra

Balance, proportion and elegance are the predominant characteristics of classical music. During the middle years of the eighteenth century, immediately prior to the full flowering of classicism in music, a profusion of orchestral music was produced at the great courts of Europe such as at Esterhazy (Haydn), Mannheim (Stamitz) and for the public concerts at, for example, the *concerts spirituels* in Paris. As well as establishing how to write for the various instruments of the orchestra as it was then made up, it was during the latter half of the eighteenth century that the classical forms of sonata, symphony, string quartet and solo concerto were developed. The four-movement symphony reached its zenith in Haydn's last 12 symphonies known as the 'London Symphonies', in Mozart's last three symphonies, numbers 39, 40 and 41, and in Beethoven's first two symphonies. Beethoven, a pupil of Haydn, was content to use the same instrumentation as in Haydn's grandest symphony, number 104, for his first two symphonies though the scoring is fuller for the wind instruments. If you are going to offer orchestration in the exam you should now set about studying some of these works, paying particular attention to how the various instruments are used, both singly and in combination.

The classical orchestra grew out of the mid eighteenth-century court orchestra which consisted of two oboes, two horns, strings and continuo, with bassoons doubling the bass part and trumpets and drums added ad lib. Only the orchestral parts were published and the continuo part was realised from the bass part by the composer. It was essentially a three-part texture with the oboes and violins carrying the melodic material, horns sustaining in the middle register and bassoons, viola, cello and bass providing the bass line. A comparison with the scoring of Haydn's last symphony in 1794, number 104 known as the 'London', shows how the texture changed throughout the Classical era. Notice in particular:

- the replacement of the harpsichord (continuo) with orchestral sounds providing the harmonic in-filling
- the more idiomatic use of the wind instruments, now comprising two flutes, two oboes, two clarinets and two bassoons.

The clarinet was a late addition and its use in the symphonies of Mozart and Haydn was infrequent. The horns and trumpets, still melodically limited by being valveless, reinforce and sustain the harmonies in the middle register. In the string section the most noticeable difference is in the liberation of the viola from its subservience to the bass line and its contribution to middle register texture. Trombones are not found in classical symphonies.[2]

---

2   However, Mozart used them to good effect in his religious and operatic music.

Classical: Orchestration

In the exam

The exam question is an exercise in the appropriate scoring of one or more extracts from a classical symphony. The amount to be scored will not be excessive for the time available. In order to complete the working you will need to know:

- the harmonic vocabulary specified on page 8;
- the working compasses of instruments commonly used in the classical orchestra;
- the clefs and transpositions used for each instrument;
- the conventions for setting out an orchestral score.

The original scoring will be specified and the requirement is to score the extract(s) from a piano reduction.[3] The success of the orchestration will be determined by its appropriateness rather than on how closely it replicates the composer's original scoring. There are several ways of scoring a piece of music and it will be the accuracy of the scoring and stylistic awareness shown that will influence the assessment.

Question: From the piano reduction of an extract from the Finale of Symphony no. 103 in E♭ by Haydn score the extract for 2 flutes, 2 oboes, 2 clarinets in B♭, 2 bassoons, 2 horns in E♭, 2 trumpets in E♭, timpani in E♭ and B♭ and strings. See Example 7 for the original scoring.

Example 1

---

[3] Although piano reductions are usually written on two staves, in the exam 2, 3 or 4 staves may be used.

Example 2   Haydn Symphony no. 103 in E♭, Finale (excerpt)

Classical: Orchestration

A few hints

- When orchestrating from a piano reduction it is often necessary to reinforce the texture in the middle register; Haydn uses horns and trumpets to do this. In the classical period the key in which a horn played could be altered by attaching lengths of tubing called 'crooks'. Composers would write all horn parts in the key of C major and then specify the key of the horn that was to be used. Example 3 shows some of the common transpositions.

  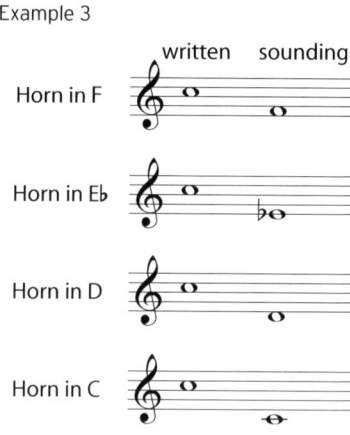

  Example 3

  Note that horn in C sounds an octave lower than written. If the horn parts are in B♭ it is common to specify whether this is B♭ alto – where the horn sounds a tone lower than written, or B♭ basso – where the horn sounds an octave and a tone lower than written.

  Beware – if the horn part is written in the bass clef the horn in C sounds as written and the transpositions work upwards, so that the horn in D sounds a tone higher than written, the horn in E♭ a minor third higher, and so on.

- As with horns, the trumpet parts were also written in the key of C. However, to confuse matters, unlike the treble clef horns, the transpositions work upwards. Thus, the trumpet in C sounds as written: the trumpet in D one tone higher, the trumpet in E♭ (as in the extract) a minor third higher, and so on until we reach the trumpets in A and in B♭ where the transposition works downwards so that the trumpet in A sounds a minor third lower and the trumpet in B♭ sounds a tone lower than written.[4]

- The transpositions for the clarinets in A and B♭ were always indicated by the use of key signatures, as in the Haydn extract where the key signature of F major for the B♭ clarinet indicates that the actual pitch is that of the key one tone lower, that is E♭ major. The choice of which instrument is to be used is based upon the avoidance of keys using many sharps or flats.

- Another aspect of orchestrating from a piano reduction is the need to double notes, usually notes common to a succession of harmonies – binding notes, the use of which helps avoid grammatical error in elementary harmony. Care is needed, however, not to disturb the harmonic balance and most often the root or fifth of the chord are the preferred choices.

- Octave and unison doubling also needs consideration, particularly with regard to tone colour and idiomatic use of the instrument in question. Generally, octave doublings of wind instruments, apart from oboe and clarinet, are satisfactory, though much depends on register. The flute in its lowest register is orchestrally ineffective and the oboe in its top octave loses its characteristic tone colour. (There is a good discussion of these aspects in Gordon Jacob's *Orchestral Technique* in the chapter on Woodwind and Horns and students are advised to study this.[5])

- The extremes of register are not encountered in eighteenth-century scoring and the upper limits, as a working rule, of three octaves above middle C for the violin, two for viola and one for cello should be more than adequate, with written G above middle C for the double bass. Natural and artificial harmonics and other special effects such as *sul ponticello* and *col legno* belong more to nineteenth- and twentieth-century instrumentation. It was not normal to mark phrasing in eighteenth-century parts, only essential bowing. It is worth noting in the Haydn extract how the viola begins by doubling the cello part but breaks free to play in sixths with it: also how the double bass is silent before it reinforces the cello entrance with the theme. Indeed, effective scoring relies very much upon the use of rests to point and help shape the phrasing.

- The range of the hand-tuned timpani, or kettle drums, in use in the classical period was an octave, divided into overlapping intervals of fifths as shown:

  The two notes used were the tonic and dominant of the keys of the movements being played. Rolls were indicated by either 𝄾 or 𝆒. The timpani were used most often in conjuction with trumpets, particularly at climactic cadences. When scoring the excerpts in the exam, thought needs to be given to the dynamics and the balance of sound.

---

4 In this respect they resemble the transpositions for the clarinet in A and the clarinet in B♭.
5 Gordon Jacob, *Orchestral Technique* (Oxford University Press)

Classical: Orchestration

- When writing chords, the usual spacing for the woodwind is for the flutes to take the top parts, followed by the oboes and then the clarinets and bassoons with each instrument's part clearly defined. The later practice of dovetailing the woodwind parts to create a blended sound is not commonly found in eighteenth-century scoring.
- The most important factor in scoring from a piano reduction is the ability to grasp the overall musical significance and from this to determine what is important and what is not and to reflect this in the scoring.

Exercises – *see overleaf for original scoring*

1. From the piano reduction of an excerpt from the second movement of Symphony no. 1 by Beethoven, score in an appropriate manner the following excerpt for 2 flutes, 2 oboes, 2 bassoons and strings:

Example 4

2. From the piano reduction of an excerpt from the second movement of Symphony no. 1 by Beethoven, score in an appropriate manner the following excerpt for 2 flutes, 2 oboes, 2 clarinets in C, 2 bassoons, 2 horns in F, and strings.

Example 5

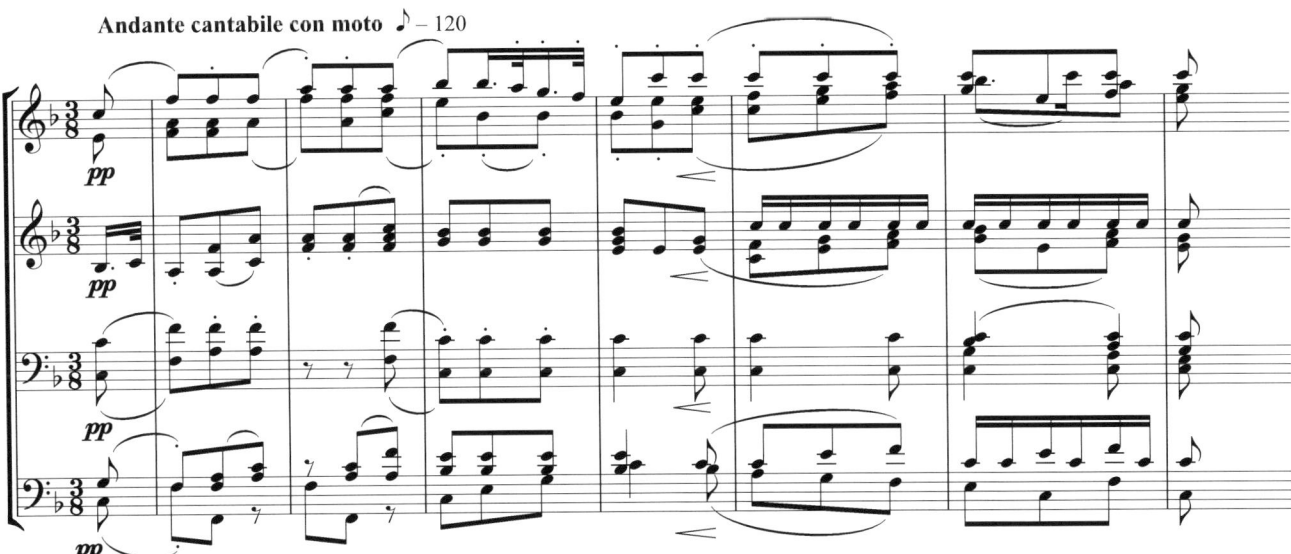

Classical: Orchestration

Original scoring for Examples 4 and 5.

Example 6 — Beethoven Symphony no. 1, second movement (excerpt)

Example 7 — Beethoven Symphony no. 1, second movement (excerpt)

Period 3: Early Romantic

The following general consideration of the harmonic idiom of the period investigates material by Schumann and Mendelssohn. Then follows a more syllabus oriented discussion of material by Schubert.

Nineteenth-century harmony

There is a sense in which it is true to say that nothing new was introduced into harmonic vocabulary during the nineteenth century. A careful check in a book such as *The Oxford Harmony*, Volume 2,[1] will show that examples of all the more 'advanced' chords can be found in music written earlier than the nineteenth century. What was new was the way in which these chords were used. Usually the function of non-diatonic chords in music by baroque and classical composers was decorative; rarely, if ever, did such chords create tonal ambiguity for more than a moment or two. When we turn to the nineteenth century we find that as well as being used as decorations of straightforward progressions, these chords are sometimes treated as essential, for example as a chromatic pivot to enable a smooth modulation to a remote key.

To clarify, in order to succeed in the following assignments you should be completely fluent in the use of all the harmonic vocabulary that is derived from triads and the sevenths, ninths and thirteenths that are extensions of triads; also all the chromatic chords included in advanced textbooks.

Now, consider the following example from Schumann's *Fantasiestücke* op. 12 no. 3, 'Warum?'

There are various ways in which you might analyse this short piece but before you do so, if you possibly can, play it through several times so that you are fully aware of how it sounds.

---

[1] H K Andrews *The Oxford Harmony Volume 2* (Oxford University Press). Now, sadly, out of print, but copies may be found in libraries or obtained from second-hand book dealers.

Early Romantic

Example 1   Schumann *Fantasiestücke* op. 12 no. 3, 'Warum?'

16

Now look at bars 1-4. The purpose of the beginning of a piece of tonal music is to establish the tonality – in this case D♭ major. How is this done? Could you say for sure that bar 1 is pointing in the direction of D♭ major? No – the harmony is a second inversion of the dominant seventh of A♭ major that moves quite conventionally to the root and fifth of the tonic of A♭ in bar 2. But wait a moment – the beginning of the second bar has only an empty fifth; on the second half of the first beat, when the chord is filled out, as well as the third, C, there is a G♭, contradicting the G♮ of the first bar. Thus we have another dominant seventh and the way towards D♭ major is made smooth.

So much for harmonic analysis of these bars. Now look at the melody; a simple rising scale, tonic-supertonic-mediant in D♭ major. It is simple and unambiguous.[2]

We have just investigated a typical example of nineteenth-century harmony; the vocabulary is no different from that of Haydn and Mozart – or Bach and Handel for that matter. What is significantly different is the way in which the vocabulary is used. We might call this a difference of style. If you intend to answer the question on early romantic harmony you must learn the ways in which composers of that period used harmonic and melodic resources. Study of harmony at this level requires considerable time spent getting to know in detail music from the period in question. This is in addition to knowledge of basic chords and chord progressions required for graded exams in theory. You are now working at a considerably higher level than that.

Now look on to bars 14-16; they comprise a straightforward perfect cadence in D♭ major, the key whose initial establishment we have just discussed. Keeping the tied top F as a binding note, Schumann makes a movement towards a perfect cadence in C. Notice how, at the beginning of bar 18, he once again withholds the third: it is not clear at this point whether the music is major or minor. He then moves straight on to cadence in F minor (which he *does* make clear on the first beat of the bar).

F minor is, of course, one of the keys closely related to D♭ major (relative minor of the dominant), but what of the relationship between D♭ and C majors? The flattened supertonic, D♭, is the root of the Neapolitan chord in C. At a more elementary level this chord is learnt as a first inversion. As you explore the nineteenth-century repertoire you will find it occurs quite often in root position.

Try playing from bar 14 and finish with a chord of C major at the beginning of bar 18. Then try the same thing with a chord of C minor at the end. The latter is unconvincing whereas the former is quite satisfactory. Albeit briefly, Schumann modulates from D♭ major to F minor through C major, and although his purpose was by no means to furnish students of the twenty-first century with examples of harmonic progressions, it serves as a useful example here.

It is not within the scope of this book to enumerate all the chromatic chords and illustrate their uses by nineteenth-century composers. You will find 'stock' progressions in harmony textbooks but you need to go further than these and discover for yourself how the various chords were used by such composers as Schubert, Schumann, Mendelssohn, Chopin and their contemporaries. You should explore the repertoire for yourself, with the guidance of your teacher, and compile your own anthology of examples which you play, analyse, memorise and write from memory, thereby making the harmonic moves part of your personal musical experience. They need to become as much part of your musical thinking as scales and arpeggios are in your practical technique.

As you do this you will also be starting to absorb the styles used in piano works of this period, thereby preparing you for the particular questions that will be set in the section of the paper that deals with early romantic harmonic style.

---

2   The melody is decorated, but you should be able to distinguish between the prevailing direction of a melody and decorative diversions.

Early Romantic

Before we move on to a practice question, have a look at the first of Mendelssohn's *Lieder ohne Worte*, op. 19 no. 1.

Example 2   Mendelssohn *Lieder ohne Worte* op. 19 no. 1 (excerpt)

The tonic key is clearly established in the first two bars and when the 'song' begins there could be nothing more clear-cut than the phrase which steps down the scale from subdominant to tonic. Then a brief visit to the dominant followed by an even briefer glimpse of the supertonic minor–relative minor of the subdominant. The final bass note of bar 4 is the raised leading note of F♯ minor and with a tonic seventh (in F♯ minor) at the end of the first beat of the next bar we are set up for a classic II7-V7-I in E major. At the end of bar 5 the 'song' has quavers B and A. The first of these two notes may be heard as an appoggiatura but equally well may be heard as an essential note, making the chord IV9. It is less important to decide between these possibilities than it is to allow the overall effect of the music to soak into your musical memory; within the space of two bars Mendelssohn has used a succession of straightforward harmonic moves in an equally straightforward texture. However he has created a richness by compressing into such a short span of time the glimpse of F♯ minor, which is immediately denied, then the mild clash between the bass A and melody note B leading to a gently sighing Ic-V imperfect cadence.

As you continue with your studies of this period and style you should pay as much attention to harmonic rhythm and texture as you do to chord progressions. They are linked inextricably.

Writing for Pianoforte

An example of a piece of piano music, part of a movement from an incomplete sonata by Schubert follows (Example 3, overleaf). A quick glance will show that this is a ternary structure and you have to provide part of the B section. The left-hand clefs have been omitted so that you may feel free to write in whatever octave seems best. However, you should not infer that you *must* have the left hand in the treble register at some point. Bars 44-48 are left completely blank for you to devise an approach to the return. Cover the original scoring, Example 4, on page 21 and see how you get on.

Early Romantic: Pianoforte

Example 3

Schubert Sonata in E, D. 157, Minuetto (excerpt)

How did you maintain interest during the various repeated patterns? So as to retain the dance-like character of this minuet it would be unsuitable to use extensive passages of a complex contrapuntal nature; they would be out of place in the third movement of a sonata of this period.

One very common cause of ambiguity in exam answers is the careless use of accidentals. This exercise requires you to think carefully about the inflection of notes, beginning straight away in bar 21. What is the A♮ telling you? Whether or not you jumped into the minor form of F♯, which the continued use of the raised leading note in bars 22, 24, 25 etc, should lead you to suspect to be the key, you must give some thought to the repeated use of A♮ in bars 21, 23, 25 and 26. You might have considered putting these bars in D major, but if you use this key then how do you explain the appearance of G♯ in bars 22 and 24? It *can* be explained, but not in a very straightforward way, and straightforwardness is one of the characteristics of this minuet.

Now look carefully at how Schubert manages this passage (Example 4). Yes, D major does feature very fleetingly. Notice how he builds the tension from bar 25 through to bar 29. Notice also the similarities between the section from bar 30 and what he wrote from bar 21.

The repetition of bars 38–40 in bars 42–44 is a commonplace occurrence and serves to decrease the tension as well as prepare for the stock formula in bars 47 and 48 through which Schubert reaches the third section of his ternary structure.

As a supplementary exercise you could set yourself the task of writing the third section of this movement – either give yourself the top line or, better still, write the whole thing. It may not be strictly according to the syllabus but it will help you to understand the style of the period, and that is the real purpose of your studies. If you have gained a thorough grasp of the styles used by the composers of the early decades of the nineteenth century then you will be able to deal with whatever material you encounter in the exam.

You and your teacher should be able to devise further practice material given the examples in this guide. Be assured that the exam paper will not ask you to write more than is reasonable within the time available. In your preparation you may well work on longer passages than might be completed in about 35 minutes – there is so much more to musical study than practising the snippets selected for exam papers.[3]

Example 4

Schubert Sonata in E, D. 157, Minuetto (bars 21–48)

---

[3] You are strongly advised to practise material of the right length towards the end of your preparation. One of the surest routes to a low mark is to mis-manage your time in the exam.

Period 4: Twentieth Century

There are two possibilities for you in this period and you may choose to complete either or both of them. The pre-requisites for these two aspects of 20th century music differ considerably as the following material makes clear.

Popular Song

As with almost all the other options in this section of the exam it is assumed that you already have a thorough grounding in harmony and counterpoint. Now you need to apply your knowledge in the context of this particular style. If you look through some examples of this genre you will quickly realise that very often the piano accompaniment includes the vocal part. Writing in this way is not a problem as far as consecutive octaves are concerned. They are idiomatic to this style. If you have learned your harmony thoroughly you should have no difficulty understanding this.[1]

Although you will be using 'S Wonderful as an exercise you can make good use of the material to observe some important stylistic features.

- The piano part is an accompaniment, not an equal of the voice. There may well be some independence in the accompaniment and in particular this may happen while the singer dwells on a long note or during interludes between phrases (see bars 7 and 8). A skilful writer will integrate such detail into the overall style of the song.

- The chord symbols provide only a sketchy outline of what happens in the realisation and you will need to exercise considerable ingenuity and craftsmanship to produce a musically acceptable working of the passage set in the exam.

- You may wonder how to decide how many notes to have at any one place. There are no rules to follow apart from your general sense of style. Study as much repertoire as you can[2] and you should develop a feel for this important matter. Try to think pianistically and not regard this as a part-writing exercise.

Now let's attempt the exercise on Gershwin's 1927 song, 'S Wonderful. The entire refrain is given and after you have tried the exercise in this form you will be able to make alternative exercises.

Although the refrain is intended to be repeated and the original has a first time bar as well as a second time, only the second time version is given. There is a section of the melody for you to complete and elsewhere sections for piano. In the last four bars the whole show is yours.

---

1   But in case you do, the reason is that consecutive octaves are a fault only when the individuality of parts is compromised. A passage that is supposed to be in four distinct parts, such as a chorale, would be deemed faulty if two of those parts were identical – even if only briefly.

2   As always this means play and sing the music as well as analyse it.

Twentieth Century: Popular Song

Example 1

Music and Lyrics by George Gershwin and Ira Gershwin *'S Wonderful*

© 1927 (renewed) Chappell & Co Inc and New World Music Co Ltd, USA
Warner/Chappell Music Ltd, London W6 8BS
Reproduced by permission of International Music Publications Ltd
All Rights Reserved.

Notice the similarity between bars 1-8 and 9-16 in Example 2. Always with such similarities there is the issue of how much use to make of the earlier material. You may have done as Gershwin did and use as much as possible, but equally you could do something different in bars 9-16. The important thing is how authentic and consistent the style of what you have written is (always assuming you have written music that realises the chord symbols).

A great variety of ways of ending the song are possible and it is unlikely that your melody will closely resemble Gershwin's unless you know this song already. What do you make of the 'inner part' in bars 31 and 32 (G G F E♭) in Example 2? Neither G nor F is part of the chord of A♭ major but this little extra adds a piquant touch to the end of the song. Such additions are not prohibited; far from it. If you can do this sort of thing effectively it will help raise your mark in the exam.[3]

An extra exercise would be to allow yourself only bars 1 and 2 in full. Thereafter give yourself only the voice part and chord symbols. This is a much bigger task than you will be given in an exam but will be good practice for you. One thing to look out for is the change of style from bar 17 to the reprise at bar 25. Such changes are commonplace in this kind of music.

---

[3] Such additions must be effective, stylish and not distort the music. Here it is the final cadence that is given added harmonic colour; in another song opportunities may present themselves at an earlier point.

Twentieth Century: Popular Song

The field of popular song is very big and Example 3 comes from a different part of the century. You don't need to know the whole story of how *Joseph and The Amazing Technicolor Dreamcoat* came into existence in order to work Example 3, nor even to know that the music was written for young performers. It is a very popular work and you may have taken part in a performance yourself. If you know the music and can write out the missing parts from memory, well and good. Be assured that you will be awarded very high marks if you do this in an exam.

This is a rather longer task than you will be given in an exam, but there is no harm in that. As a hint, where you have to supply the voice part from the upbeat to bar 17 the piano part does not double it very much. Be guided in this matter by what you find at the beginning of the music. As in the exam, you have to write the ending in full.

Example 3   Lyrics by Tim Rice, Music by Andrew Lloyd Webber: 'Joseph's Dreams' from the musical *Joseph and The Amazing Technicolor Dreamcoat*

Twentieth Century: Popular Song

© Copyright 1969 The Really Useful Group Ltd, London
All Rights Reserved. International Copyright Secured.

Twentieth Century: Popular Song

Ways in which the piano part may include notes other than those contained in the chords given in the symbols have already been discussed. This happens straight away in this section of 'Joseph's Dreams'.

Your first decision is whether to make bars 5-8 an exact repeat of the opening. As with the Gershwin, exercise, it is not wrong to do something different, but the music must always conform to its context. Notice that in bar 12 the original has another embellishment of the specified chord. Before that, notice that although the accompaniment largely shares the same rhythm as the voice part, in bars 9 and 11 there is a bit of extra movement which counterpoints the even notes of the voice part.

The chords from bar 17 follow a very simple descending sequence and it would be unusual if the voice part were not to do likewise. However, as with the earlier point regarding the use of material from bars 1-4 in bars 5-8, it is not automatically wrong if your voice part here is not sequential. A very strong justification for the sequence is the phrase structure of the words. A sequential treatment will underline this structure and it is usually a good thing if the music enhances the words rather than undermines them.

Example 4   Lyrics by Tim Rice, Music by Andrew Lloyd Webber: 'Joseph's Dreams' from the musical *Joseph and the Amazing Technicolor Dreamcoat*

© Copyright 1969 The Really Useful Group Ltd, London
All Rights Reserved. International Copyright Secured.

There are literally thousands of songs readily available that you can use to practise writing in this particular style. If your copies lack chord symbols then you can easily add them. Whatever you write, make sure that it is pianistic and that chromatic elements move smoothly, especially in slower music. Finally, no matter what style you are studying, you have not finished an exercise until you have played your music through so you really know what it sounds like. If on the play through you are not satisfied, work at adjusting the music until you are completely happy. Examiners need to be convinced that candidates can 'hear' what they have written and that they can judge the style of their composition from the page.

Melodic Composition

The ability to write a coherent melodic line based on a given opening suited to the particular characteristics of the instrument/voice chosen is a challenge of a different sort from those of the other questions in Section A, all of which involve harmonic and tonal considerations. In this question, the focus is on melody and rhythm, relying on the devices of sequence and varied phrase structure within a dynamically conceived whole.

Music relies more heavily than any other art form on varied repetition, since it exists in a time continuum and the use of sequence (from the Latin verb *sequor* meaning 'to follow') is one of the most frequently used methods of continuity. For example, both melodic and rhythmic sequences can be seen at work in the shortest of pieces: in the English traditional melody *Barbara Allen*, the persistent rising and falling thirds and the ♫ ♩ rhythm of the opening phrase dominate the song. A sequence occurs in bars 5 and 6 (though not an exact one), but the coherence of the melody results from the melodic and rhythmic cells that fuse into an arch-like structure:

Example 5 Traditional *Barbara Allen*

Further examples of this process of cellular structure can be seen in the following examples from Bartók's *Mikrokosmos*:

Example 6 Bartók *Mikrokosmos* (excerpt)

© Copyright 1940 by Hawkes and Son (London) Ltd. [Definitive corrected edition © Copyright 1987 by Hawkes and Son (London) Ltd.]

Note the importance of the falling fourth and the effectiveness of the rhythmic variation and varied phrasing.

In the next example, again from Bartók's *Mikrokosmos*, continuity is achieved by the use of inversion (not exact, but sufficient to register) and by fragmentation of the opening phrase:

Example 7 Bartók *Mikrokosmos* (excerpt)

© Copyright 1940 by Hawkes and Son (London) Ltd. [Definitive corrected edition © Copyright 1987 by Hawkes and Son (London) Ltd.]
Reproduced by permission of Boosey and Hawkes Music Publishers.

Phrase structure is of paramount importance in melodic writing since it is the means of giving significance to these related units of sound. While most statements require an answer, it is not always the classically balanced phrasing that is the most telling:

Example 8 Bartók Violin Concerto no. 2, 2nd movement (excerpt)

© Copyright 1941 by Hawkes and Son (London) Ltd. Reproduced by permission of Boosey and Hawkes Music Publishers.

Here, the opening statement is answered by an upward-moving phrase related in its use of the interval of the fourth and semiquaver rhythmic figure. The third phrase, irregular in its length, grows out of the two opening balanced phrases and, in its wide sweep, extends the range but with hints of the semiquaver rhythm and the interval of the fourth.

In a less exalted way, the phrase structure of the second half of the United Kingdom's National Anthem is similar. The irregular phrasing of the English folk song *Searching for Lambs* is another example of the freedom and sweep that the organisation of melodic germ cells into forward moving phrases can impart:

Note how the melodic phrase of the first bar is present in bars 3, 5 and 6 without being consciously sequenced and is now part of a flowing line.

Example 9 Traditional *Searching for Lambs*

When studying the given opening melodic phrase, determine whether it is based on a defined pattern of notes related to a scale or mode, or whether its interest lies in its intervallic relationships. For example, a given opening such as in Example 10, would obviously suggest a pentatonic continuation.

Example 10

The five notes of this ancient scale can best be visualised as being drawn from the scale of C major with the third (E) and seventh (B) omitted. This series can begin on C, D, F, G and A and then be transposed to any tonic. The black keys of the piano can afford easy access for pentatonic extemporizations.

On the other hand, the given opening may suggest the whole-tone scale or one of the modal scales, such as the Lydian mode of the Bartók Violin Concerto extract. (The Lydian mode is the major scale with the fourth degree raised a semitone.) The opening bars must be seen only as the starting point for melodic invention and there is no need to stick rigidly to a scale or mode if such is identified, though it will obviously colour what you write.

The dynamics, tempi indications, changes of register and expressive shaping should be integral and interwoven in the overall mood(s) of the composition. Thought should be given to the sound characteristics of the chosen instrument/voice and a good way of preparation would be to write pieces for a particular performer with whom you work, from whom valuable insights can be gained regarding effective register and particular sound characteristics when rehearsing and performing the piece. Be responsive to the mood of the given opening material as well as to its rhythmic and melodic potential, exploiting features which seem significant. Of the many models that could be cited *Danse de la chèvre* by Honegger is an accessible and effective piece for solo flute and well worth studying from a compositional point of view, as are the *Six Metamorphoses after Ovid* for oboe by Benjamin Britten.

In the exam a fragment of melody will be given and candidates must continue this to create a coherent and complete short piece of music of 24 to 30 bars. The fragment will be taken from a twentieth-century work which is not diatonic: to answer this question successfully candidates will need to use some other system than tonal harmony as a basis of their work.

One such system is the twelve-note method or serial technique developed by Schönberg and his pupils Berg, Webern, Krenek and others. In an attempt to destroy any vestige of tonality the 12 semitones of the octave are used to create a tone-row wherein no one note is pre-eminent, that is, no one note is repeated within the row. The row can be inverted, worked backwards (retrograde) and the inverted row can also be retrograde. The original row and its three derivatives can also be transposed making in all 48 possible statements.

Taking the three notes of the opening of Peter Maxwell Davies' 'Recitando' from *The Kestrel Paced Round the Sun* for solo flute (Example 11), a twelve-note tone row can be constructed. Shown below are the tone row and its inversion, retrograde and inverted retrograde derivatives. The resultant melody for viola (Example 12) is based on these and concludes with a restatement of the original row, slightly modified with octave substitutions. In designing the tone row, opportunities for use of sequence were incorporated (notes 4, 5, 6 sequenced by notes 7, 8, 9) and, of course, both retrograde versions return the series to its starting note and this can be used rhythmically to achieve a sense of conclusion if so wished.

Example 11

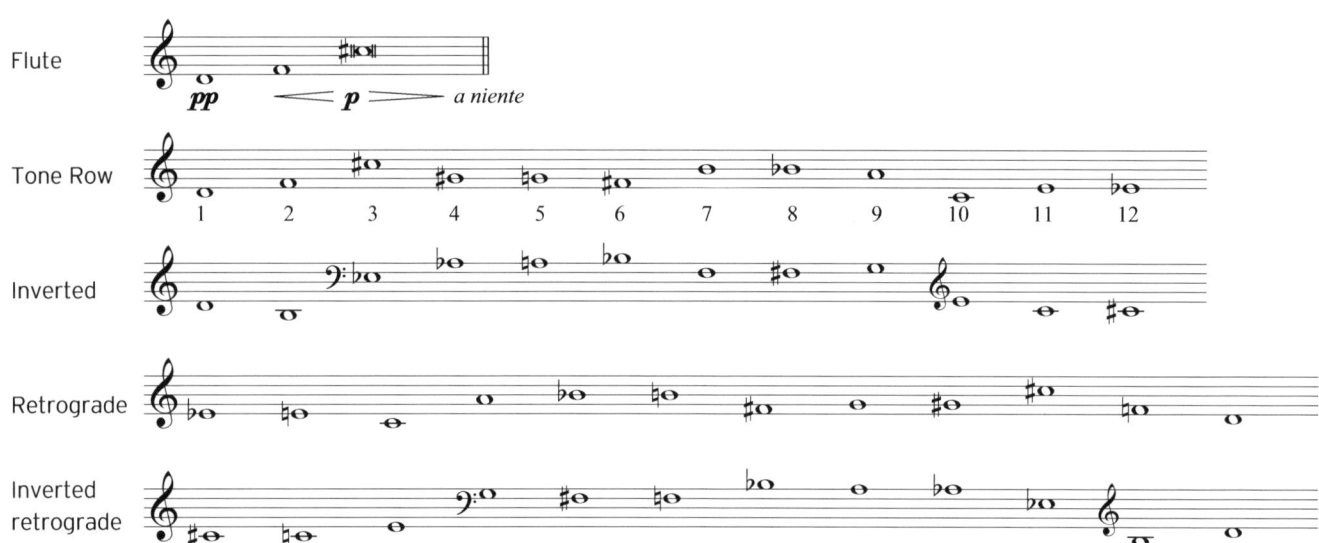

Example 12

A piece of this nature will rely heavily upon rhythmic invention, phrase shaping, dynamics, tempo change and varied articulation, perhaps more so than the previous examples, and while at first it might appear a rather mechanical means of melodic extension the system can be the basis of both expressive large-scale compositions, such as Berg's Violin Concerto, and small-scale compositions such as those by Webern.

Twentieth Century: Melodic Composition

Example 13

Peter Maxwell Davies *The Kestrel Paced Around the Sun*, Recitando

© Copyright 1976 by Boosey and Hawkes Music Publishers Ltd. Reproduced by permission of Boosey and Hawkes Music Publishers.

Twentieth Century: Melodic Composition

Maxwell Davies did not, as will be seen (Example 13), develop the opening notes into a tone row; instead the concentrated on intervallic relationships, particularly the opening interval of the third and the overall interval of the seventh, and its inversion, the second. He also extends the opening phrase to both a major and minor ninth[7] when recalling the opening. The extremes of register are exploited and devices such as variable ligatures (1) indicating small rubato-like fluctuations of tempo, and notes in parenthesis (2) indicating the notes to be played 'aside', as it were, contribute to a sense of flight and of movement suggested by the title. Two other sections, the Andante and the Allegro, both related to the Recitando intervallically, make up the first movement of this work. At figure (3) of the Andante the ♪ sign indicates a tapped key note. The Allegro, through use of contrasting dynamics, trills and rapid runs suggests more frenzied movement and the repeated Ds of the final two lines of the music act as pedal notes heralding the dying away of the music, thus making, structurally, a satisfying whole.

Examples

The following melodic openings, of the kind that will be set in the exam, suggest a variety of treatments and should be developed (c. 24-30 bars) for a particular instrument or voice which must be stated. Candidates may transpose the chosen opening to a suitable register for the nominated instrument or voice.[8]

Bartók Chromatic Invention (2) no. 92 from *Mikrokosmos* vol. 3

The continuation of this opening is given in Example 7. Compare your working with the original.

Bartók In Lydian Mode no. 37 from *Mikrokosmos* vol. 2

Bartók Whole tone scale no. 136 from *Mikrokosmos* vol. 5

© Copyright 1940 by Hawkes and Son (London) Ltd. [Definitive corrected edition © Copyright 1987 by Hawkes and Son (London) Ltd.] Reproduced by permission of Boosey and Hawkes Music Publishers.

---

7   The intervals are referred to here by their conventional names (e.g. major/minor ninth) even though there is no such thing as major and minor in non-diatonic music.

8   Make sure that you remember to state the instrument or voice for which you are writing. It is a vital part of the assessment.